For Gemk,

Whose endless supply of ideas and honest critique made this possible.

感謝 Gemk

源源不絕的靈感及誠懇的建議讓這一切成真。

Oliver the Otter
水獺大偵探

Coleen Reddy 著

衛欣、王鶯 繪

薛慧儀 譯

三民書局

This is Oliver Otter.

He looks like an ordinary otter but he isn't.

He is a detective.

Oliver is fishing. Fishing is his hobby.

2

這位是水獺奧利佛，
他看起來和普通的水獺沒兩樣，
但其實他可是一點兒也不普通喔！
他是個偵探。
奧利佛這會兒正釣著魚。
釣魚是他的嗜好。

"Excuse me, Mr. Otter," says a voice. "Can I speak to you?"
Oliver turns around and sees an ostrich.
"How can I help you?" asks Oliver.
"I heard that you are a good detective," says the ostrich.
"I need you to find my eggs. I hatched three eggs yesterday.
But when I woke up this morning, my eggs had disappeared.
They have been stolen. Can you help me?"

「對不起，水獺先生，能不能和你談一下？」有個聲音說。

奧利佛轉過頭，看見一隻鴕鳥。

「我能幫你什麼忙嗎？」奧利佛問。

鴕鳥說：「聽說你是個很不錯的偵探，我想請你幫忙找回我的蛋。
昨天我還在孵的三顆蛋，今天早上一醒來，它們就不見了。
它們被偷走了！你能不能幫幫我呢？」

"Sure," says Oliver. "Show me where your nest is."
The ostrich leads Oliver to her nest, which is under a tree.
The nest is empty.
When the ostrich sees the nest, she starts crying.

6

「沒問題！」奧利佛說。「讓我看看你的鳥窩在哪裡。」
於是鴕鳥便帶著奧利佛去察看她在樹下的鳥窩。
鳥窩裡真的是空的呢！
鴕鳥一看到空空的鳥窩，就哭了起來。

"Don't cry," says Oliver. "I'll find your eggs for you."
Oliver looks around and sees an owl sleeping in the tree.
He yells at the owl to wake it up.

「別哭。」奧利佛說。
「我會幫你把蛋找回來的。」
奧利佛觀察了一下四周，
看見一隻貓頭鷹在樹上睡覺。
他對著貓頭鷹大叫，想把牠給叫醒。

The owl wakes up and screams,

"What do you want? Can't you see that I'm sleeping?"

"I'm sorry to disturb you," says Oliver.

"Did you see anything odd last night?"

"No," says the owl. "But I could smell something odd.

I smelled oranges. There are no orange trees around here

so I thought it was odd."

10

　　貓頭鷹被吵醒了，牠大喊：「你想做什麼？沒看到我正在睡覺嗎？」
「對不起打擾了，」奧利佛說，「你昨天晚上有看見什麼奇怪的事情嗎？」
「沒有，」貓頭鷹說，「但是我聞到一種奇怪的味道，那是柳丁的味道。
　　　　　　因為這附近沒有柳丁樹，所以我覺得很奇怪。」

"Oranges?" repeats Oliver.

Then he starts searching the ground around the nest.

He takes out a magnifying glass and looks around very closely.

「柳丁？」奧利佛重複了一遍。
然後他開始在鳥窩四周的地面上搜查。
他拿出一個放大鏡，看得非常非常仔細。

"AHA!" screams Oliver.
"What? Have you found my eggs?" asks the ostrich.
"No," says Oliver. "I found orange peels."

「啊哈！」奧利佛叫了出來。
「怎麼了？找到我的蛋了嗎？」鴕鳥問。
奧利佛說：「不是，我找到了柳丁皮。」

15

"I know of an ogre that loves oranges.

I'm sure that he took your eggs," says Oliver.

"How can we find this ogre?" asks the ostrich.

"We'll just follow the trail of the orange peels," says Oliver.

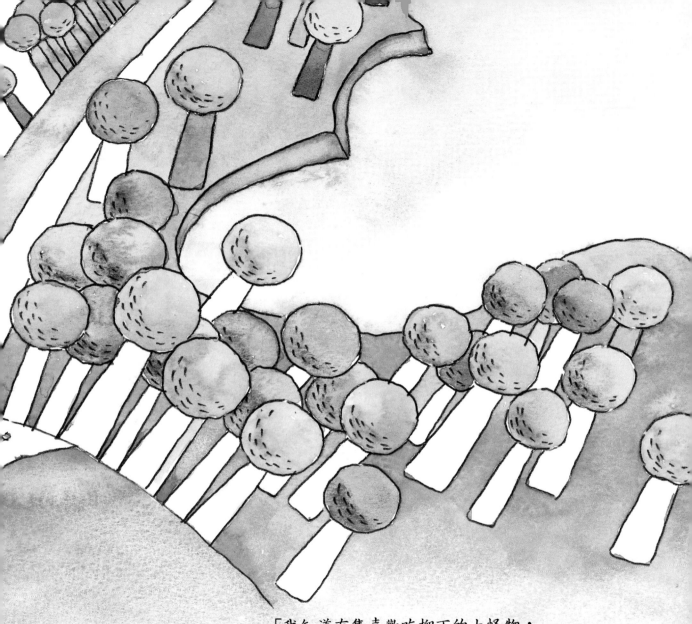

「我知道有隻喜歡吃柳丁的大怪物，
我相信就是他把蛋拿走了！」奧利佛說。
「要怎麼樣才能找到這隻大怪物呢？」鴕鳥說。
「我們只要一路跟著柳丁皮走就可以了。」奧利佛說。

Oliver and the ostrich follow the trail of the orange peels through a forest.

The trail stops outside a house.

"The ogre and your eggs are in that house," says Oliver.

Oliver and the ostrich slowly creep up to the house.

They peep in through the window and find that the ogre isn't home.

They go into the house.

　　奧利佛和鴕鳥一路跟著地上的柳丁皮，
穿過了一座森林，最後在一棟房子外停下來。
「大怪物和你的蛋就在這房子裡面。」奧利佛說。
　　奧利佛和鴕鳥躡手躡腳地走近這棟房子。
他們從窗戶外向房子裡偷看，發現大怪物不在家。
　　　　　　　　　　　於是他們便走進房子裡。

In a corner of the house, there are many ostrich eggs.

"How will you know which eggs are yours?" asks Oliver.

The ostrich replies, "Mothers always know."

She picks up three eggs.

在屋內的一個角落裡，有好多好多鴕鳥蛋喔！
奧利佛問：「你要怎麼知道哪些蛋是你的呢？」
鴕鳥回答說：「媽媽總是有辦法知道的。」
於是她撿起了三顆蛋。

21

Just then, they hear a noise.

They turn around and find that the ogre has returned. He looks really mad.

"What are you doing in my house?" yells the ogre. "These are MY eggs!"

就在這時候，他們聽見了一陣怒吼。
他們回頭一看，發現大怪物已經回來了！他看起來好生氣好生氣喔！
「你們在我家做什麼？」大怪物大喊著：「這些都是我的蛋！」

"Ogres don't lay eggs," says Oliver. "You've been stealing ostrich eggs. These eggs belong to this ostrich and we're taking them back."

"I own those eggs. They're mine," says the ogre.

「怪物又不會下蛋！就是你，一直在偷鴕鳥的蛋！」奧利佛說。
「這些蛋是這位鴕鳥媽媽的，我們要把蛋帶回去。」
「那些是我的蛋！它們是我的！」大怪物說。

25

Then the ogre starts crying.

"I'm so lonely," cries the ogre. "I was going to wait for the eggs to hatch and then take care of all the little ostriches. They would not have hated me. They would have loved me. Then, I wouldn't be lonely anymore."

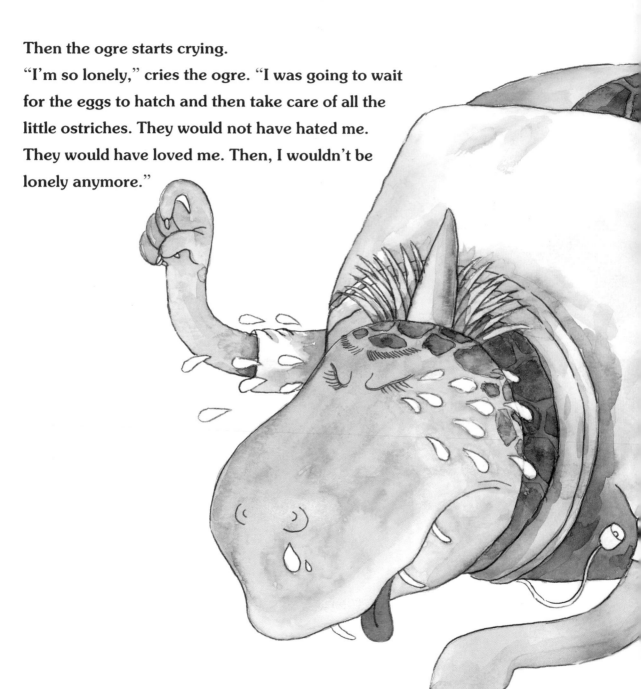

然後怪物就哭起來了！

「我好寂寞嘛！」大怪物哭著說。「我想等到這些蛋孵化，

然後照顧所有的小駝鳥。他們不會討厭我。

他們會很愛我，那麼我就不會寂寞了。」

"Really?" asks Oliver.

"No, not really," says the ogre as he bursts into laughter.

"You silly otter! You'll believe anything! I'm going to sell these eggs at the market and make a fortune!"

"Look, oranges!" screams Oliver.

The stupid ogre turns to look and Oliver and the ostrich quickly run out of the house.

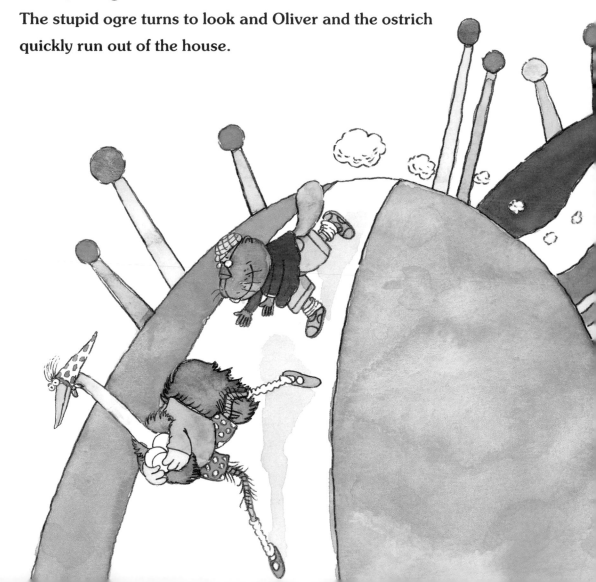

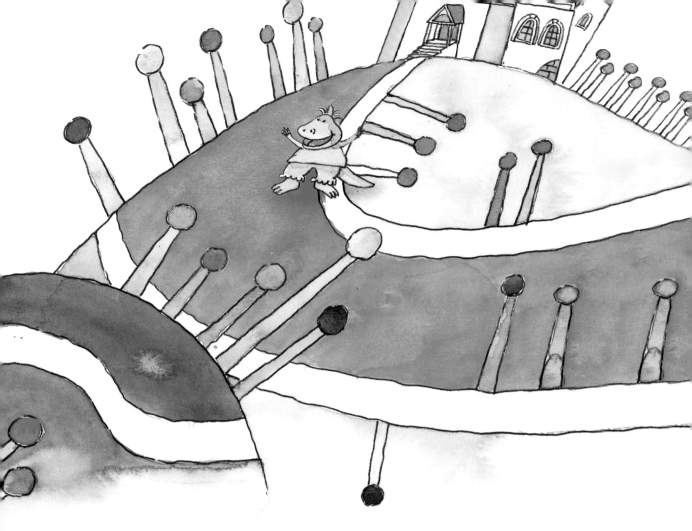

「真的嗎？」奧利佛問。
「哈！才怪！」大怪物說著，突然大笑了起來。
「笨水獺！我說什麼你都會相信！
我要把這些蛋拿去市場賣掉，然後賺一大筆錢！」
奧利佛突然大喊一聲：「看！柳丁！」
笨怪物一回頭看，奧利佛和鴕鳥便趕快趁機逃出了屋子。

The next day, Oliver reads an article in the newspaper:

"An ogre was seriously hurt today when some alligator eggs that he had stolen hatched and attacked him. The alligators were returned to their mothers and the ogre is still in hospital. The ogre said that he thought the eggs were ostrich eggs."

There is a picture of the little alligators attacking the ogre. The ogre finally gets what he deserves!

30

第二天，奧利佛在報紙上看到一則新聞：
「今天有隻大怪物受了重傷，因為他偷的鱷魚蛋孵出小鱷魚來，
還狠狠地攻擊了大怪物。小鱷魚們目前已被送回他們的媽媽身邊，
大怪物則還在住院休養中。怪物表示，他以為那些蛋是鴕鳥蛋！」
報紙上還有一張小鱷魚攻擊大怪物的照片。
這隻大怪物總算得到他應有的報應了。

大家一起來尋蛋

哎呀！鴕鳥媽媽的蛋又不見了，可是水獺大偵探出國度假去了，鴕鳥媽媽到底該怎麼辦呢？大家快來幫幫忙，替鴕鳥媽媽找回她心愛的寶貝蛋兒！

（自己玩的時候，不可以偷看答案喔！）

工具　一個骰子。

原點

1. 拼出「水獺」，然後前進三步，否則不動。

2. 唱一首歌。

3. 學大怪物的叫聲。

4. 水獺用了什麼東西找到柳丁皮？
（答對不動，答錯退兩步）

5. 親爸爸或媽媽一下，親了之後，再進五步。

6. 拼出「貓頭鷹」，然後前進一步，否則不動。

7. 做鬼臉。

8. 水獺休閒活是什麼
（答對不動，答錯退一

9. 再擲次骰子

32

11. 你不小心被柳丁皮絆倒，退後三步。

12. 大怪物偷了幾顆鴕鳥媽媽的蛋？
（答對不動，答錯退一步）

13. 遇到好心的小仙女幫忙，前進四步。

14. 和你身旁的人猜拳，贏的話往前走一步，輸的話往後退兩步。

15. 對某個人說「我愛你」，說了之後，前進兩步。

）. 請爸爸或媽媽親你一下，親了之後，前進兩步。

20. 恭喜你找到了鴕鳥蛋，記得給自己一個愛的鼓勵喔！

16. 被大怪物攻擊，身受重傷，回到原點。

17. 表演一項特殊才藝。

18. 水獺大偵探回國，幫你找到了鴕鳥蛋，前進到終點。

19. 拼出「鴕鳥」。
（答對前進一步，答錯退兩步）

生字表

12. 三隻鴕鳥 19. ostrich

8. Fishing is his hobby.（釣魚是他的嗜好。）

答案：1. otter　4. magnifying glass（放大鏡）　6. owl

34

全新創作 英文讀本
帶給你優格（yogurt）般‧青春的酸甜滋味！

Teens' Chronicles

愛閱雙語叢書

青春記事簿

大維的驚奇派對／秀寶貝，說故事／杰生的大秘密
傑克的戀愛初體驗／誰是他爸爸？
叛逆大維打工記／外星老師來上課／耶！放假了！

附中英雙語CD
（共八冊）

適讀年齡：10歲以上

你我身上純真的影子，
透過一篇篇幽默風趣的故事重現，
推薦你這套青春無悔的創作系列，
讓愛玫、杰生、大維、凱爾、海倫、傑克，
帶你進入他們的世界，品味另一種學習英語的全新感受。

國家圖書館出版品預行編目資料

Oliver the Otter:水獺大偵探 / Coleen Reddy著;衛
欣, 王鶯繪; 薛慧儀譯.－－初版一刷.－－臺北
市; 三民, 2003
　　面;　　公分－－(愛閱雙語叢書.二十六個妙朋
友系列) 中英對照
　ISBN 957－14－3764－6　(精裝)

　1.英國語言－讀本

523.38　　　　　　　　　　　　　92008800

© **Oliver the Otter**
──水獺大偵探

著作人　Coleen Reddy
繪　圖　衛　欣　王　鶯
譯　者　薛慧儀
發行人　劉振強
著作財
產權人　三民書局股份有限公司
　　　　臺北市復興北路386號
發行所　三民書局股份有限公司
　　　　地址 / 臺北市復興北路386號
　　　　電話 / (02)25006600
　　　　郵撥 / 0009998－5
印刷所　三民書局股份有限公司
門市部　復北店 / 臺北市復興北路386號
　　　　重南店 / 臺北市重慶南路一段61號
初版一刷　2003年7月
　編　號　S 85648－1
　定　價　新臺幣壹佰捌拾元整
行政院新聞局登記證局版臺業字第〇二〇〇號

ISBN　957－14－3764－6　（精裝）